A CHARLIE BROWN THANKSGIVING™

BY CHARLES M. SCHULZ

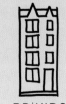

RP|KIDS

PHILADELPHIA • LONDON

Printed in China

9   8   7   6   5   4   3   2
Digit on the right indicates the number of this printing

ISBN 978-0-7624-3303-2

Art adapted by Tom Brannon
Design by Frances J. Soo Ping Chow

Running Press Book Publishers
2300 Chestnut Street
Philadelphia, PA 19103-4371

Visit us on the web!
www.runningpress.com
www.Snoopy.com

Lucy always held the football for Charlie Brown to kick—and she always pulled it out from under him!

"It's Thanksgiving. She wouldn't try to trick me on a traditional holiday!" Charlie Brown said as he charged at the ball.

But Lucy yanked it away and asked, "Isn't it peculiar, Charlie Brown, how some traditions just slowly fade away?"

CAN YOU ADD SOME STICKERS TO THE SCENE?

"Holidays always depress me," Charlie Brown said as he checked the mail.

"I know what you mean!" replied his little sister, Sally. "Why should I give thanks on Thanksgiving? What have I got to be thankful for? All it does is make more work for us at school!"

USE YOUR STICKERS TO DECORATE THE SCENE.

"Thanksgiving is a very important holiday. Ours was the first country in the world to make a national day to give thanks. What are you going to do on Thanksgiving, Charlie Brown?" Linus asked.

"Sally and I are going over to my grandmother's for dinner," replied Charlie Brown.

WHAT'S OUTSIDE?
SHOW US WITH YOUR STICKERS.

RING! RING!

"Hi, Chuck? This is Peppermint Patty. My dad said I could share Thanksgiving with you, Chuck! And remember that kid Marcie? She's going to join us, and Franklin, too. See you!"

"Three guests for Thanksgiving and I'm not even going to be home!" moaned Charlie Brown.

"You simply have two dinners," Linus said calmly. "Cook the first one yourself for your friends and then you go to your grandmother's with your family for the second one."

WHAT'S IN CHARLIE BROWN'S LIVING ROOM?
ADD STICKERS TO DECORATE.

Charlie Brown's dog, Snoopy, was ready to help. First, he set up a table and lots of chairs in the backyard.

"Okay, Snoopy, that's pretty good," Charlie Brown said. "Come on inside—we need some help with the food."

CAN YOU HELP SNOOPY DECORATE WITH YOUR STICKERS?

The kids set up an assembly line to make Thanksgiving dinner. Charlie Brown and Linus put bread in the toasters. When the toast popped up, Snoopy spread butter on it.

Then Snoopy raced around the kitchen, making popcorn and filling bowls with jellybeans, potato chips, and pretzels.

Soon everyone arrived. It was time for Thanksgiving dinner!

USE YOUR STICKERS TO HELP SNOOPY COOK.

"Before we are served, shouldn't we say grace?" asked Peppermint Patty.

Linus stood up. "In the year 1621, the Pilgrims had their first Thanksgiving feast. Elder William Brewster, who was a minister, said a prayer that went something like this: 'We thank God for our homes and food and our safety in a new land. We thank God for the opportunity to create a new world for freedom and justice!'"

"Amen!" Peppermint Patty said.

COMPLETE THE SCENE BY USING YOUR STICKERS.

On each plate, Snoopy proudly placed two slices of toast, a pile of popcorn, a handful of pretzels, and lots of jellybeans. Then he sailed each plate down the table like a Frisbee!

"What blockhead cooked all this?" Peppermint Patty asked angrily, when she saw the funny food. "Don't you know anything about Thanksgiving dinner?" Charlie Brown got up from the table and sadly walked away.

USE YOUR STICKERS TO HELP SNOOPY SERVE DINNER.

"You're kinda rough on Charlie Brown, weren't you, sir?" Marcie asked.

"Rough? We were supposed to be served a real Thanksgiving dinner!" replied Peppermint Patty.

"Sir," asked Marcie. "Did he invite you for dinner, or did you invite yourself, and us, too?"

"I never thought of it like that," Peppermint Patty admitted. "Marcie, maybe you can go to ol' Chuck and patch things up for me?"

ADD SOME STICKERS TO COMPLETE THE SCENE.

Marcie found Charlie Brown inside. "Don't feel bad, Chuck, Peppermint Patty didn't mean all those things she said."

"I just feel bad because I ruined everyone's Thanksgiving," said Charlie Brown.

"But Thanksgiving is more than eating, Chuck," Marcie said. "We should just be thankful for being together!"

Peppermint Patty peeked into the room. "Apologies accepted, Chuck, ol' boy?"

"Sure!" Charlie Brown said.

WHAT'S GOING ON INSIDE?
SHOW US WITH YOUR STICKERS.

"Good grief, it's four o'clock!" Charlie Brown said. He called his grandmother and told her that all his friends were still there, and that none of them had eaten dinner yet. So she invited everyone to Thanksgiving dinner at her house!

"Hooray!" cheered the Peanuts gang. They piled into the station wagon and began to sing, "Over the river and through the woods to Grandmother's house we go!"

DECORATE THIS SCENE WITH YOUR STICKERS.

Back at Charlie Brown's house, Snoopy and Woodstock decided to celebrate Thanksgiving on their own—with a turkey dinner and all the trimmings!

HAPPY THANKSGIVING!

USE THE REST OF YOUR STICKERS ON THIS PAGE.

p. 3

pp. 4-5

pp. 6-7

pp. 8-9

pp. 10-11

pp. 12-13

pp. 14-15

pp. 16-17

pp. 18-19

pp. 20-21

p. 22-23

p. 24